Peppercorn's Magic

A live Stage Comedy or Story Book for Children

Script and Lyrics by Florence Novelli
Music by Bernard A. Aaron

To order additional copies of this book, contact:
Xlibris
UK TFN: 0800 0148620 (Toll Free inside the UK)
UK Local: 02036 956328 (+44 20 3695 6328 from outside the UK)
www.xlibrispublishing.co.uk
Orders@ Xlibrispublishing.co.uk

ISBN: 978-1-9845-9552-2 (sc)
ISBN: 978-1-9845-9553-9 (e)

Print information available on the last page

Rev. date: 07/21/2020

Peppercorn's Magic

A Live Stage Comedy or Story Book for Children

Script and Lyrics by Florence Novelli
Music by Bernard A. Aaron

(approx. one hour performing time)

Characters:

PEPPERCORN (Leprechaun)
PRINCESS
JOLLY OLD KING
TROLL

Musical Sequence

"We Were So Happy" ....(Princess's song)

"I'm a Jolly Old King"...(King's song)

"I Come from a Land of Moon Drops" ....(Peppercorn's song)

"Ha! Ha! Ha!" .... (Troll's song)

"For Gold Will Never Buy You a Friend"...(Peppercorn to Troll)

"We Are Jolly Old Friends" ....(Finale Song... full cast)

Castle Interior

Lights up on Castle interior. King and Princess prepare for party. Princess is placing garlands around a royal pedestal. She stands back in admiration.

PRINCESS

Doesn't that look gorgeous, Father?

(King is half way up small ladder attaching streamer to wall. His crown is askew. He strains to hook one end of decoration and turns to look at princess. His crown topples to floor. He reaches for it but slips and falls with a bump.)

KING

Help!

PRINCESS (*rushing to aid*)

Father! You should be more careful. Are you alright?

KING (*reaching for crown*)

Yes, yes. I'm fine. Stop fussing and help me up. This is no position for the King of Not-at-All to be caught in.... falling flat on my... er..."dignity" as it were! I suppose I'm getting old. Every year I find it harder and harder to prepare for our party. All this up and down. This is woman's work anyway... so much silly fussing. Next you'll have me in an apron.... Helping the royal cook!

PRINCESS

Don't be grouchy, Papa! Perhaps you've been working too hard. Here.. . let's sit down and rest awhile.

(She helps king to throne.)

You must be in your best mood for the Prince. Oh, Father! I'm so excited! Everything looks so lovely.

KING *(taking her hand in his)*

I'm sorry, my pet. I know this is a very special year for you, and for me too... with your prince coming to ask for your hand in marriage. I'm very happy for you, my lovely child. But I'm a little sad too, for soon there will be wedding bells. Your handsome young prince will carry you away from your old father to be his queen in some far off land.

(Lights dim and off-stage rumbling is heard.)

PRINCESS

Father.. . listen! It's that ugly old troll from under the bridge. Oh! I wish he would go away! Sometimes when I'm happy and everything is going so well, I get a scared feeling deep down, that it can't last... that perhaps in some way that troll will spoil it all.

KING

Nonsense, my dear! Don't bother your pretty little head about him. Every fairytale kingdom such as ours has a troll. They like dark places, but if we stay away from his cave, he won't bother us... I hope. Now, what was I saying? Ah. yes. . . about your prince...

PRINCESS

You're right, Father. We shouldn't let our fear of that ugly troll spoil our party. Oh, Papa... I don't want you to be sad about my marriage to the prince. When I'm his queen... why not make him the new King of Not-at-All? For, as you say, you are getting old now and have no son to carry on as King.

KING

I think that is a very good idea. .. of mine. Then you would be Queen of Not-at-All... just as your beautiful mother was. You know, we are lucky people to have so much joy and beauty in our lives. Besides, I don't have a mother, a sister or a brother. All I have is you, my gumdrop. You're my dearest treasure. My love you could not measure.

(King and princess join hands and twirl around merrily.)

PRINCESS (kissing father on forehead)

You'll always be my very special dear old papa! Come. . . I want you to see all the delicious food the royal cook is preparing for the party.

KING

Oh no! You don't get an apron on me, my little lady!

PRINCESS

You don't have to do any cooking. Just smell and look
Come along, now.

KING

No cooking?

(Princess shakes head.)

No baking?

(Princess shakes head.)

No frying ?... nothing? Well... maybe a little tasting?

(Princess shakes head. King turns to audience.)

KING

Don't you think the king is entitled to a taste of his
own tea-time goodies?

(Audience response)

PRINCESS

No tasting! Well...maybe just a lick.

KING

Alright, my little cookie.

(He reaches for ladder.)

I might as well take this out, since the servants won't.

(End of ladder catches a garland, dragging it behind.)

PRINCESS

Father! Look out! What will I do with you? So clumsy! So fat!

KING

Not "fat"! Portly, my dear. Now please show a little respect for the king. After all, you're not the Queen of Not-at-All yet, you know.

PRINCESS

But Father. .. Look what you've done!

KING

Oh! Dear! Well, never mind

(He leans ladder against wall.)

It won't take us long to put it up again. I'll hold the ladder for you, my dear.

(Lights go off and on. Rumbling is heard, louder Sound of Troll's laughter. Stage darkens. Troll is seen flitting around. Does not speak, just laughs wickedly, stealing whatever he can and putting all into a large sack.)

TROLL

Ha! ha! Hee! hee!

PRINCESS

Father! It's that ugly old troll. He's stealing everything! Oh! Stop him! Someone stop him!

(*She sits and weeps.*)

KING

Stop it, you ugly little thief! Stop it, I say!

TROLL

Ha! ha! Hee! hee!

(*He continues laughing, knocking things over, and taking whatever he likes. He then moves to exit. King follows gingerly. Lights flash. Thunder rolls. Troll turns around to king. He shouts out*) Boo!

(*King retreats. Troll follows threateningly.*)

And next time it will be two "Boo"s! Ha! ha!.... Ha! ha!

(*Troll exits. Lights to black.*)

End of Scene

SCENE TWO

Same

Lights up on castle interior. It is dismal. princess is crying whilst decorating with paper garlands. She ties a gartand to the wall. It falls. She picks up some old remnants and tries to arrange them. They don't look good.

PRINCESS

It's no use. How can I make it look beautiful with these silly old things? I don't want to try any more. Everything is as ugly as that ugly old troll.

(She flings down garlands. King enters humming to tune of his song "I'm a Jolly Old King". He looks around.)

KING

Well, well, well! It is beginning to look very nice my little bumble bee.

(He moves to throne and sits down.)

PRINCESS *(weeping)*

Oh! Father! How can you act as though nothing has changed. You know it is ugly and we are so poor now.

I think it is silly to prepare for a party when we really have nothing to be happy about.

(Princess goes to king, sits at his feet and sighs.)

If only Mr. Peppercorn were here. He would make everything alright again... I know he would.

KING

Come, come now, my little tear drop. I'm not happy either My heart is broken like an old violin. But there is enough sadness among our people, and have they not throughout my long and happy reign always known me as "The Jolly Old King"? So, my dew drop. we must have this party... just as we do every year. Our people have been waiting for months. They will not starve, because the little gold I had left in my treasury, I shared among them. So come, my dream drop, let us speak no more of this Pickle Pepper.... Peter Pickle... or, Popcorn.. .

PRINCESS

Mr. Peppercorn

KING

Or whatever his name is. He is just a fantasy... and fantasies are of no use to us now. It is too late for wishes and dreams of magic and all such nonsense.

PRINCESS

It is never too late for wishes and dreams I don't ever want to be that old.

(During introductory music chords to Princess's song, she narrates)

Let us wish for happy things; Ice cream swirls and golden rings

(She then sings)

<u>"We Were So Happy"</u>

(PRTNCESS)

1) We were so happy, father and I;
   O such stateliness marching by;
   The royal crown upon his head;
   The joy he felt that I would wed;
   Alas for shame, our glee was lost;
   Whenever that cruel troll had tossed:
   Our riches from the kingdom cherished;
   Now they're gone, forever perished.

2) Help me children, one and all;
   Catch that star, don't let it fall;
   And let us wish for happy things;
   Ice cream swirls and golden rings;
   I feel a little glow inside;
   Building up, it cannot hide;
   Look it shows upon my face;
   Sadness gone, leaves no trace.

3) Is it magic in the air?
   Yes I feel it. Don't you there?
   Let us leave its spell unbroken;
   Casting goodness, words unspoken;
   Words unspoken.

KING *(Sighs lovingly)*

> Well, I can't make your wish come true, my little princess, but I can give you something that is real.
>
> *(King exits. Princess improvises excitedly with audience.)*

PRINCESS

> What can it be? a puppy dog? Maybe a little furry kitten?
>
> *(King re-enters with gift box and hands it to princess who hurries to unwrap it.)*
>
> What can it be?
>
> *(She takes out her sparkling crown.)*
>
> Oh! Father! My crown! You saved my crown! It is all we have left of our treasures to remind us of our happy carefree days. I shall not wear it tonight. Instead, I'll put it here....
>
> *(She places crown on window ledge.)*
>
> where all my friends can see it and take heart from its beauty. You're right, Papa. We must get ready and have our party in spite of the ugly old troll.
>
> *(She looks at king who now looks sad.)*
>
> My dear father. You have made me feel so much better' But now you look sad. Why?

KING

> Oh! It is hard to feel light when inside I'm feeling so heavy. And besides.. .. You're standing on my foot!

(He steps backwards but trips and falls into large wicker basket, legs kicking in the air.)

Help! Help! I did it again! Help me out of this basket!

(Princess invites children on stage. They help to pull king from basket. She thanks them and they return to seats.)

PRINCESS

Oh! Father! Really! I don't think you will ever change no matter what happens... and I really wouldn't want you to.

(She kisses him on forehead.)

Help! Help! Come on now, cheer up. After all, we still have each other don't we?

KING

You're right, my sugar plum. I will try.... for am I not a 'jolly old king"?

(Music intro plays. King sings his song.)

"I'm a Jolly Old King"

(KING) (refrain)   I'm a jolly old king with a dilly and a dally;
And a chuckle and a smile and a ho! ho! ho!
I'm a jolly old king with a giggle and a gurgle;
Singing fa-la-la, and away we go.

1)   Fiddle-faddle feathery, fancy and free;
Bumbling, fumbling, happy as can be;
A basketful of royalty, noisy as a loon;
Music maker come, strike up a merry tune.

(repeat refrain)

2)   Dancing and prancing, light upon my feet;
Ladies they exclaim: "Oh my! What a treat!"
My long royal robe and my crown on top;
But what am I saying, now let me stop.

(refrain)

3)   I'm not a rich king as all of you can see;
Tattered and ragged, I'm ashamed as can be;
My belly 'tis so, it is round like a pie;
But makes a good pillow, should ever she cry'

(refrain)

PRINCESS

> Papa, you're wonderful. But in spite of all our efforts, the palace still looks bare and cold.

KING

> Well then, what we need is a jolly warm fire!
>
> *(King cups hands to mouth and call out)*
>
> Royal woodcutter!

KING

> Royal cook!

PRINCESS

> He's busy in the kitchen

KING

> Royal dog catcher!!

PRINCESS

> He's gone to the dogs.
>
> *(King grumbles to himself.)*

KING

> Oh, alright. I'll do it mysell I have to do everything around this castle
>
> *(He exits, denouncing the servant situation.)*

PRINCESS *(to children)*

You believe in magic, don't you?

(response)

Well, I'm sure you know that leprechauns are the greatest magic makers in the whole world. They are everywhere, you know. Have any of you ever talked to a leprechaun? Now, Mr. Peppercorn.... he is a very special leprechaun. .. I guess because he's the only one I know. He lives in our forest behind the castle. That would be the same as your park or garden. I go there often to visit him, but he is not always there. Only sometimes, when I am sad and lonely, and he hears me crying.... Then.... Poof! There he is! Do you know what? (audience response) Mr. Peppercorn paints all the rainbows over the sky....and at the end of each one, he leaves a glittering pot of gold.... just for good luck! He told me that whenever I am sad, I should look for a rainbow, and then I would be happy again. Oh! I must bring Mr. Peppercorn here now to paint me a lovely holiday rainbow. But I need your help, boys and girls. I know that Mr. Peppercorn will like all of you. We have to wish for him all together as hard as we can. But first, we must say the magic words:

Ripperty rapperty, ripperty ree;
Please, Mr. Peppercorn, please come to me;
Snowflakes and moonbeams, honey and spice;
Paint me a rainbow of colours so nice.

(With eyes closed, Princess repeats magic words one line at a time, waits, then on opening eyes and seeing no one there, she again turns to children.)

Again, boys and girls, louder this time- We must make
him hear us

(They all shout out magic words, but to no avail.
Princess sighs.)

It's no use. The ugly old troll has taken everything....
maybe even Mr. Peppercorn! Oh! Wouldn't that be
awful! What would we do?

(She moves to stage front and sits down, drooping her
head sadly. Lights dim. Green spot on Peppercorn as
he enters. He tip-toes around princess, but she does
not notice.)

PEPPERCORN (*in Irish accent, to children*)

The princess can't see me just yet because she's not
sure. She's so unhappy that she doubts me magic to
appear. I knowl (He looks around.) If she wants to see
me, she'll have to touch the star in her crown. That,s part
o' me magic. You know who I am... don't you? (children's
response) That's right. Me name is Mr. peppercorn.

(Music intro plays. Peppercorn sings his song.

"I Come from a Land of Moon Drops"

(PEPPERCORN)   1)   I come from a land of moon drops;
                      Where laughter and fun float by;
                      On fleecy white humps and lemony tops;
                      Parading the rainbow sky.

                2)   Close your eyes and believe in me;
                      Or I will leap away;
                      For I am happy and I am free;
                      To frolic, skip and play.

3)   'Tis true I'm tiny and hard to find;
I'm only seen by few;
But let me help you ease your mind;
And be as lucky too.

(Verse 4 is spoken to soft music background.)

4)   Peppercorn here, Peppercorn there;
Peppercorn, Peppercorn everywhere;
I can appear before you can blink;
And vanish as soon as you wink.

(singing resumes for verse S.)

5)   Piccalty hiccalty talagaboo;
Star dust to sprinkle on you;
Leap over mountains, come and try;
Riding moonbeams way up high'

(Repeat verse 1 to end song.)

(Princess does not respond. Peppercorn turns to audience.)

I guess you're going to have to help me. I'll count to three' then we'll all shout: "Touch the star in your crown!"

(Peppercorn counts. Everyone shouts together' Princess turns to audience.)

PRINCESS

Touch the star in my crown? What for?
(There is a magical music chime as she touches star:)
Oh! Mr. Peppercorn! You really are here!

PEPPERCORN

Sure now. And what would you like to be doing today' me little princess? Slide down a rainbow? Or go to the wishing well with me?

PRINCESS

Oh, Mr. Peppercorn, that would be fun but not right now. I'm too unhappy It's all so terrible. The ugly old troll from under bridge has stolen all the kingdom's riches It's almost our party time. I must find the finest rainbow ever' because at its end, I know there'll be a sparkling pot of gold that we can share with everyone Oh! You will help us, won't you?

PEPPERCORN

Sure now, and I know just the rainbow for you. Made it myself. 'Tis the finest and brightest of colours. Been after savin' it for a special occasion...like this one here.

PRINCESS

Mr. Peppercorn, it sounds like a wonderful rainbow. ... but we should hurry. Without the pot of gold, our kingdom will be sad forever.

PEPPERCORN

Well now, we'll be getting the pot o' gold, and I hope it'll be makin'yer all happy. Now.... if I can just remember where I put it.

(Peppercorn, followed by princess, leaves stage and goes through audience aisles, searching.)

Now let me see....

(They exit back of house. Roll of thunder is heard. Enter Troll. He narrates verse one of "Troll's Song" menacingly to sustained drum roll, without melody.)

"Troll's Song"

TROLL   1)   Rattlesnakes, owl's eyes, rolls of thunder;
                     Plague the kingdom with blight and plunder;
                     Crown jewels, banquets, chests of treasure;
                     No more shall reign such royal pleasure.

(Four tonic chords of intro music plays during which troll paces to and fro'. He then sings verses 2 and 3, each with four chord intro.)

    2)   Ha! ha! ha! Ho! ho! ho!
          I am up from my cave below;
          Watch me dance and delight you all;
          I have a charm ten giants tall.

    3)   Mischievous joker that I am;
          Ready to grab your jellies and jam;
          Have you a Penny or a bowl of stew:
          Watch it go "poof!"... the bad troll too

    4)   I snarl and growl and rage like a bear;
          Pacing the ground and pulling my hair;
          Where or where is that Pot of gold?
          Tell me, my poppets, just show me the road

(After four chord pacing, music stops and Troll narrates verse 5 lo sustained drum roll.)

    5)   Peppercorn thinks he's so smart;
          But I can fool him, watch me start;

His magic can't fight my power,
When I lurk in the dark at tonight's late hour!

(Verse 2 is repeated without intro, then four chords strum intro to finale verse 6.)

6) And now I return to my lair in the ground;
   Leaving you all with a rumbling sound;
   My anger churns, my vengeance burns;
   I'll be back... .... .. Boogaloosack!

Fiddlesticks and fiddlestones! Aching backs and broken bones! Bother! Bother! Bother! Curse the leprechaun and all his magic! I'm more powerful than he. I have the riches.

(He notices crown on window ledge.)

Ha! ha!.... The princess's crown I see.

(grabs crown)

Hee! hee!.... And now I do have everything!

(He leers and gloats at crown, then paces.)

But wait now.... I thought I heard them talking about a pot of gold. Tell me, children, where have they gone to find this pot of gold?

(audience response,)

Eh? Eh? Come on now, be my friends and tell me. Ha! ha!

(King's voice is heard approaching, singing his song.)

Quick! I shall hide. Maybe I can find out where the princess and that silly leprechaun have gone. Shhhh! Shhhhhhhh! Don't telt the king!

(He crouches behind throne. King enters carrying a pile of logs. He weaves and strains. Logs wobble, but he manages to stack them down near hearth.)

KING

Phew! Now we'll have a grand fire to warm us in no time

(pauses and looks around)

Where has she gone?

(turns to audience)

Have you seen my little princess?

(response)

With whom? Mr. Peppercorn? No, no... that cannot be. He's just a fantasy. I bet the troll has been here!

(response)

He has? Where? Well... he couldn't have gone very far' I shall find him. and when I do I will... I will...

(boxes the air with fists)

Oh! I don't know what I'll do.

(King searches for troll but trips over logs. Audience children can see where troll is hiding and tell king. King runs off stage a tittle way into audience.)

Where did you say? Behind there?

(He points towards throne.)

Will you come with me and show me?

(He leads children from audience up on stage. As they approach troll, king cowers behind children' Troll jumps up menacingly.)

TROLL

Boo!

(King jumps back in fright. Troll chases him twice around stage. King runs with a backward slant, knees lifting high in the air.)

Ha! ha! ha! ha! I've got the crown, and I'll get the gold' I am quick, whilst you are old. You won't catch me you big fat king! I never give back anything. Ha! ha!

(Troll exits, laughing wickedly. Lights to black')

End of Scene

SCENE THREE

Castle garden (rainbow's end)

Stage black. Lights up at back of audience. Peppercorn and princess enter from rear of house.

PEPPERCORN

Now, I'm certain it was right around here somewhere.... between the sun and the moon. A darlin' spot it was.... just below the big dipper. Now, they wouldn't have moved the Milky Way on me, would they? No... there it is. .. So, the end of the rainbow must be.... right here!

(Lights up on stage. Peppercorn and princess are on stage. A bright rainbow appears with a gleaming pot of gold at one end.)

PRINCESS

Oh! Mr. Peppercorn...it's beautiful! We'll all be rich again, and the people won't have to work so hard. Oh, it looks like we shall have our happy party after all.

"So the end of the of the rainbow must be...right there!"

PEPPERCORN

    Pssst! Shhhh! Listen! I thought I heard something

PRINCESS

    What's the matter, Peppercorn? I didn't hear anything.

PEPPERCORN

    Faith in Begora! It's him ugly self!

(Enter Troll)

TROLL

Ha! Ha! So!...There is a rainbow, and there is a pot of gold!

(rubs hands and sneers)

PEPPERCORN

Be off with you...you miserable troll! The gold belongs to the darlin' kingdom of Not-at-All.

TROLL

You don't scare me, you silly little leprechaun. I am more powerful than you. Ha! ha! I shall cast a spell... Heel hee! And the gold will be all mine.

(Troll thrusts hand into cloak. On withdrawal he scatters a smoky dust.)

By all the darkness of the night; I will freeze you all with fright; As still as a rock you will remain; Until I return to this place again!

(Rubs hands gleefully)

Ha! ha!.... And that will be never! Hee! hee!

(Peppercorn and princess stand still as stone' They can't move.)

And now there's no stopping me. Hee! hee! Ha! ha!

(Troll exits with pot of gold. Enter king at a run, puffing.)

"I shall cast a spell"

KING

Oh, dear! I heard that frightful spell .. but I was helpless
to stop him.

(Noticing leprechaun, king bends down to examine him closely. Puzzled, he turns to children)

Who's that?

(On audience response, he turns to frozen princess.)

Ah! What a foolish king I have been..' not to believe in your dreams, my princess. I don't think I'll ever be happy again!

(King sits on a rock and tries to sing his song tearfully.)

I'm a jolly old king... Oh! Oh!

(Song intro replays, but changes from its major key to its relative minor key.)

I'm a sad and foolish old king!

(He stops trying to sing and turns to audience.)

What can I do to break this terrible spell?

(Improvises with children)

What was it that the troll said? Now let me see..." As still as a rock.... You will remain. ."

(With audience help, the last line is remembered')

"Until" .... "Until I return to this place again!"
Yes.... that's it! We must make him come back here!
Now let me see...

(To children)

Which way did he go?

(response)

He couldn't have gone far. Perhaps if I call?

(He shouts)

Ugly old troll!

(No response. King cups hands to mouth and shouts again, louder.)

Ugly old troll! .... I have a treasure here worth more than all the gold and wealth in my kingdom

(He listens. No response. Turns back to children.)

Perhaps he's too far away to hear me. Maybe if we all shout out together... as loud as we can. Now. .. after me. . .

Ugly old troll!

(Children shout out, but no reply. King and children shout again, even louder.)

Ugly old troll!

(Troll's voice is heard off stage.)

TROLL

Eh? What was that?

KING

Good, my friends. Very good. But now... Shhh! Shhhhh! We'll trick him.

(Enter troll)

TROLL

What treasure? Ha! ha! Where is it? What is it?

(King takes princess's hand)

KING

This, you ugly troll... this is my treasure!

TROLL

Bah! Very clever! You big fumble flab king! So ' You broke the spell by bringing me back!

(Princess and Peppercorn are coming to life again' rubbing their eves.)

But I don't care. Ha! ha! There's nothIng left that I want! Hee! hee! hee!

(Troll exits.)

PRINCESS

Oh, Father! There's no hope left Even Peppercorn seems helpless against him'

KING (sadly)

Come, my little dove. I shall take you home to the castle. I'm afraid you are right. All is hopeless now"' gone' gone' gone.. everything!

PEPPERCORN

Now just you be waitin' a minute! What sort of attitude is that for a jolly old king and a fair wee princess to be takin'? And as for myself being helpless why no! For there's a certain magic far stronger than anything on earth and that's as sure as the sun comin' up in the mornin', me darlin's.

PRINCESS

Oh, Mr. Peppercorn! What is this magic you speak of? And why have you not used it before now?

PEPPERCORN

Well now, this magic can work at any time And I would say it would be after workin' ... just about now'

PRINCESS

Mr. Peppercorn...you talk in riddles!

PEPPERCORN

Alright! Away with you now to the castle. I'll be takin' after the troll... and I'll be takin' care of him too.

(King and princess exit, leaving the leprechaun alone. Lights dim. Peppercorn walks to centre stage and turns to audience.)

(Lights to black)

End of Scene

SCENE FOUR

Troll's cave

Lights up dimly inside cave piled high with treasure in one corner. Troll sits admiring Pnncess's crown and pot of gold.

TROLL

Ha ha! Hee! hee! Just look at all this treasure. ... belonging to me!

(audience response)

Well, it's mine now!

(rubs hands in glee, pauses, then sighs.)

Mmmm... What can I do now? There's nothing left to steal. Yet somehow, I feel there is something missing. Now what can it be? Ha! I know... someone to share all this with me. Now wait a minute... I have no friends. Mmmm.... I know... I will steal some... Ha! ha!

(Troll comes out of cave and paces to and fro')

Friends. Mmmmm.... A-ha!

(Turns to children and points.)

You!... and you!... All of you! You will all be my friends! Ha! ha! And for the luck of being my friends, you will also be my slaves. Ha! ha! Slaves! What a clever troll I am! My! my! And how busy my slaves will be!... working all day and all night, for me... for me!

(He points to individual children.)

You'll wash all the dishes. You'll make the beds. You!.... you'll take out the garbage! Yes, and you'll shovel the snow. You over there! You'll clean my dirty dark old cave!

(Enter Peppercorn)

And as for you, you silly leprechaun. .. there's nothing you can do to me. I have everything. And now I have friends to work for me... hee! hee! Don't I?

(audience response)

PEPPERCORN

Friends? Ha! I see no friends. I pity you. You are a foolish old troll.

TROLL

Well, who cares? Who needs friends anyway? Not me. Ha! ha! Anyway, I can buy them. I'm rich! I can buy anything I want. I could even buy a friend... so there! Ha! ha!

PEPPERCORN

But you can't buy a friend!

TROLL

I can't?

PEPPERCORN

No. Don't you understand?

(Music intro plays. Peppercorn sings.)

"Peppercorn to Troll"

(PEPPERCORN)   1)   Ugly old troll, your wicked bad ways;
                               Won't help you on rainy days;
                               Sitting alone, not a friend by your side;
                               Wishing you did not have to hide.

                          2)   Snap yourfingers, stretch out a smile;
                               Let it grow as wide as a mile;
                               For gold will never buy you a friend;
                               As you yourself will see in the end.

                          3)   Snap your fingers, stretch out a smile;
                               Let it grow as wide as a mile;
                               For gold will never buy you a friend;
                               As you yourself will see in the end.

(At song's end, Troll shrugs his shoulders.)

TROLL

So!... I can't buy a friend. So what? I don't need them.
I have all I want... everything. Stuff and nonsense

"For gold will never buy you a friend."

Goodbye to garbage! I'm used to having no friends. Sometimes, when it's cold, I hear the people in the village laughing and sounding so happy. Bah! Stuff and nonsense! It was one of those times when I made up my mind to steal all their treasures. Bah! I bet they're not laughing now!

PEPPERCORN

Well now, they're still happy enough to be preparing for their annual royal party, me friend... even without any gold. Soon you'll be hearing their merry voices... singin, and laughin'.

(turns to audience)

Come on, children, let's ring the old troll's ears with your merry laughter.

(At children's laughter, troll puts fingers in ears.)

TROLL

I'm not going to listen. Stop laughing, everybody! Stop laughing, I say!

(Peppercorn incites more laughter from children. Then, gradually, he calms audience and turns to troll.)

PEPPERCORN

Aye! We'll be merry alright... while you'll be mopin, around here, all by yourself as usual.... with only yer gold for company. Aye! And there's a bit of a cold breeze in the air. Why, you'll be shivering here on yer own, in the dark... and the wind will be howlin' and yer bones will be rattlin'... and

(Troll interrupts.)

TROLL

Enough! Enough already! It's OK for them to be happy. They've got each other. I've got nobody!

(He begins to sniffle)

PEPPERCORN

Come now, me friend. Snap your fingers. Stretch out a smile. Return the pot o'gold.... and all the treasures. It'll make yer feel good inside. And who knows... you may get an invitation to the Party.

TROLL

Do you really think they'd invite me?

PEPPERCORN

I do. Of course... you'll have to brush up a little

TROLL

That's easy.

PEPPERCORN

And return the gold.

TROLL

That's hard

PEPPERCORN

O.K., O.K. Stay here, then and shiver in your dingy dark cave... and let the wind howl around yer, and.. .

TROLL

Wait... It's against all my thieving principles, you know. but oh, alright! I'll give it a try.

(turns to audience children)

What do you say? Do you think I should?

(response)

PEPPERCORN

That's the spirit, Mr. Troll. Aye, and I'm bound to celebrate this change of heart with a good old Irish jig.

(music accompanies leprechaun who leads troll into a short Irish jig. Dance ends.)

Now, me friend. .. away to the castle to surprise the king and princess with our good news. Follow me.

(Leprechaun and troll exit with pot of gold and riches.)

Lights to black.

End of Scene

SCENE FIVE

Castle interior

King sits upon throne, knitting. Princess helps to free him
from a tangle of wool, but becomes entangled herself.

PRINCESS

Father! You've been knitting all day. What on earth are
you making?

(King holds up a length of knitting.)

KING

A sweater for the royal Airedale, my dear

(Princess laughs, then is sad.)

PRINCESS

Oh, Papa! It's getting late... and no news at all of Mr.
Peppercorn.

KING

I'm not surprised. He's probably forgotten all about us

PRINCESS

What a terrible thing to say when he is helping us. Peppercorn is such a kind leprechaun. He's our only hope.

KING

Now now, my little bunny. I'm sure Mr. peppercorn is just fine. In fact, he may be getting rich.... sharing our gold with that troll

PRINCESS

Don't you remember what he said about having a stronger magic than any the troll may use? I have a hunch that we'll have our party after all.... and I will marry my handsome prince.... so there!

KING

I'm getting too old to trust in foolish fantasies.

(King rolls up knitting and places it in basket.)

PRINCESS

Oh! Father! You take away all hope

(Enter Peppercorn-)

PEPPERCORN

Well now.... What's this all about? No hope?

PRINCESS

Oh! Mr. Peppercorn! Weren't you able to do anything?

PEPPERCORN

Well now, me darlin' princess. Surely, you did not doubt me magic? Why.... look here!

(He indicates troll who now enters.)

TROLL

Here.

(Hands crown back to Princess,)

Take it. And I'm giving back all the kingdom's riches.... everything I stole!

(Princess and king back away a little warily.)

PRINCESS

I just can't believe it! Oh Mr. Peppercorn, that must have been the strongest magic in the whole wide world.

KING

Yes. Well, Mr. Peppercorn, this is a happy day to be sure. Let the bells ring out.... and all the good people in the kingdom of Not-at-All come to the finest and biggest party of all. Mr. Troll.... will you come too? Maybe we can be friends, now that you have been brave enough to change your ways. Tell the royal cook to serve our banquet on the gold plates!

TROLL

And on the gold cups and saucers too!

(Peppercorn reprimands him silently with a wag of his finger. Royal bells peel to herald the party, continuing to ring until Peppercorn's words of fare well.)

KING

All our hearts are full of thanks to you, Mr peppercorn. You are to be our honoured guest.... at the royal table!

TROLL

Don't forget the gold forks and spoons too... and the gold table cloths!

(Again Peppercorn admonishes him with finger wag.)

O. K., O.K Give me a little time.

(Princess turns to Peppercorn)

PRINCESS

Oh yes, Mr. Peppercorn. You have made all my dreams come true. You will always be my dearest friend. And when I marry my prince and become Queen of Not-at-All' you can come and live here in the castle with us.

PEPPERCORN

Many thanks, Princess. But I must be away to live among me own wee people in the lovely green forest. But I am always here if you look for me in your hearts.

(Everyone begins to talk excitedly about the forthcoming celebrations. Peppercorn steps forward, reaches into his pocket and sprinkles sparkle dust over everyone. They freeze. Bells pause. Peppercorn turns to audience-)

And now a word of farewell to you all. Remember, children. Keep a sparkle of laughter twinlln' in yer eyes.... your manner kind and friendly.... your words warm and wise. Then, no matter what life brings, you'll never be forlorn.

(Leprechaun scatters a handful of sparkle dust towards audience.)

A sprinkle of magic from Mr. Peppercorn!

(He then sprinkles actors who unfreeze. Music intro plays for finale song.)

KING

Oh, my! The party begins!

(Actors sing and dance.)

"We Are Jolly Old Friends"

ALL ACTORS   1)   He's a jolly old king with a dilly and a dally;
                      And a chuckle and a smile and a ho! ho! ho!
                      He's a jolly old king with a giggle and a gurgle;
                      Singing fa-la-la, and away we go.

(Actors can now dance to music only for verse 2 of "King's Song", and then sing through finale verse 2)

               2)   We are jolly old friends with a dilly and a dally;
                      And a chuckle and a smile and a ho! ho! ho!
                      We are jolly old friends with a giggle and a gurgle;
                      Singing fa-la-la, and away we go.

(End of Scene)

End of Play

Princess' Song

Words:
Brenda Katz

Music:
Bernard Aaron

1. We were so hap-py, fa-ther and I, Oh, such state-li-ness march-ing by; The roy-al crown up-on his head, The joy he felt when I would wed.

2. Help me child-ren, one and all, Catch that star, don't let it fall, And let us wish for hap-py things, Ice-cream, swirls and gold-en rings.

3. Is it ma-gic in the air? Yes, I feel it; don't you there? Let us leave its spell un-brok-en, Cast-ing good-ness, words un-spok-en.

Words:
Brenda Katz

Peppercorn's Song

Music:
Bernard Aaron

Intro. - Merry and playfully

Piano

1. I come from a land of moon drops, Where laugh-ter and fun float by;
2. ⁊ Close your eyes and be-lieve in me, Or I will leap a-way,
3. 'Tis true I'm ti-ny and hard to find, I'm on-ly seen by few.
5. ⁊ Pic-cal-ty hic-cal-ty ta-la-ga-boo, ⁊ Star dust to sprin-kle on you.

On flee-cy white humps and le-mon-y tops. Pa-rad-ing the rain-bow sky.
For I am hap-py and I am free To fro-lic, skip and play.
But let me help you ease your mind, And be as luck-y too.
⁊ Leap o-ver moun-tains, come and try Rid-ing moon-beams way up high.

D. C. (with intro.)

Spoken: (while piano plays softly)

4. Peppercorn here, Peppercorn there, Peppercorn, Peppercorn every where.
I can appear before you can blink; And vanish as soon as you wink.
Back to verse 5. whitout intro. Then, once more verse 1.

Troll's Song

Words:
Brenda Katz

Music:
Bernard Aaron

(Spoken) 1. Rattle snakes, owl's eyes, rolls of thunder, I'm a specimen of living wonder,
Handsome, debonair as any a suitor, The princess shall yet choose me to woo her.

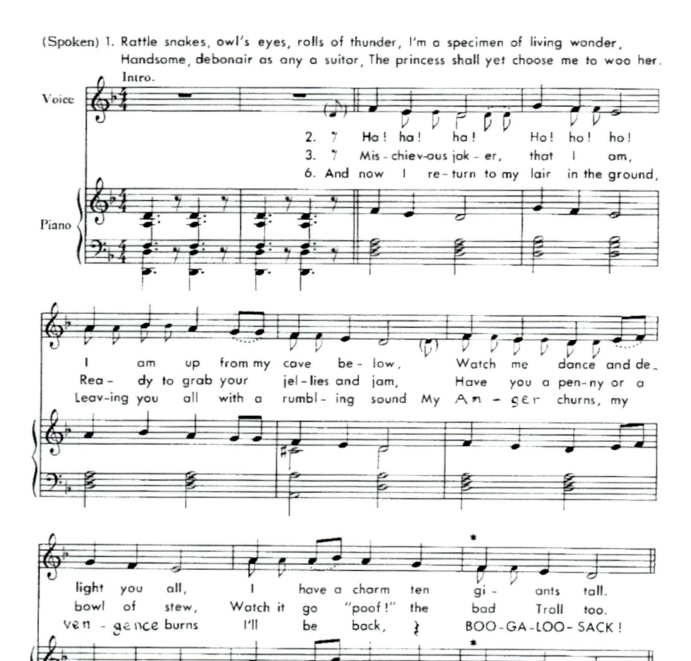

2. Ⴤ Ha! ha! ha! Ho! ho! ho!
3. Ⴤ Mis-chiev-ous jok-er, that I am,
6. And now I re-turn to my lair in the ground,

I am up from my cave be-low, Watch me dance and de-
Rea-dy to grab your jel-lies and jam, Have you a pen-ny or a
Leav-ing you all with a rumbl-ing sound My An-ger churns, my

light you all, I have a charm ten gi-ants tall.
bowl of stew, Watch it go "poof!" the bad Troll too.
ven-gence burns I'll be back, } BOO-GA-LOO-SACK!

* This bar last time very loud, letting final chord ring.

(Verses 4 and 5 on next page)

4. I snarl and growl and rage like a bear,
pac - ing the ground and pul - ling my hair; Where, oh where is that
pot of gold? Tell me my pop-pets, just show me the road!

Spoken) 5. Peppercorn thinks he's so smart, But I can fool him, watch me start.
His magic can't fight my power, When I lurk in the dark at tonight's late hour.

(Repeat verse 2 without intro;—then do verse 6 with intro.)

Peppercorn to Troll

Words:
Brenda Katz

Music:
Bernard Aaron

Voice

1. Ug-ly old Troll, your wick-ed bad ways; won't help you on
Sit-ting a-lone, not a friend by your side; wish-ing you did not

rain-y days;
have to hide.
2. Snap your fing-ers, stretch out a smile;

Let it grow as wide as a mile; For gold will ne-ver

buy you a friend; As you your-self will see in the end.

Finale

Words
Brenda Katz

Music
Bernard Aaron

CUE: — King: - - -"Oh my, the party begins." - - -

> Play Intro again, then go to verses. <

1. He's a jol-ly old king with a dil-ly and a dal-ly And a
2. We are jol-ly old friends

chuck-le and a smile and a ho! ho! ho! He's a jol-ly old king with a
We are jol-ly old friends

gig-gle and a gur-gle, Sing-ing fa- la- la and a- way we go.

If desired, the piano may play the top line again, as a conclusion.

Printed in the United States
By Bookmasters